Goodnight, Good Dog

For a certain very good dog — M.L.R.

For my lovebug — R.M.

The text of this book is set in BerhardGothic.
The illustrations are acrylic on paper.

Library of Congress Cataloging-in-Publication Data
Ray, Mary Lyn.
Goodnight, good dog / written by Mary Lyn Ray and illustrated by Rebecca Malone.
pages cm
Summary: "For one restless pup the waking world is too full of wonder to leave behind
at bedtime, until he closes his eyes and finds comfort in his dreams"—Provided by
publisher.
ISBN 978-0-544-28612-2 (hardback)
[1. Dogs—Fiction. 2. Bedtime—Fiction.] I. Malone, Rebecca, illustrator. II. Title.
PZ7.R210154Go 2015
[E]—dc23
                                2014049687

Manufactured in Malaysia
TWP 10 9 8 7 6 5 4 3 2 1
4500534871

Goodnight, Good Dog

Written by **Mary Lyn Ray**

and illustrated by **Rebecca Malone**

HOUGHTON MIFFLIN HARCOURT   BOSTON   NEW YORK

click

The dog knows the click of the lamp
when the light is turned off.

He knows the sounds the dark makes.

hmmm...

Those small night sounds.

He knows the shadows in corners of rooms.

He also knows the quiet that comes: moon quiet.

And he knows his bed, round like the moon.

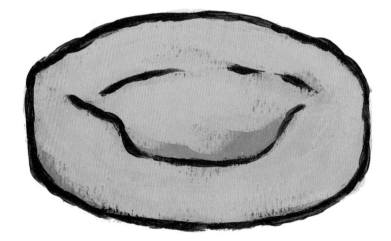

But the dog isn't sleepy.

He remembers the yellow ball of sun bouncing across the sky.

He remembers how he chased it, running in the grass.

He remembers his toys.

He remembers his dish.

He remembers words he knows—
like come

Goodnight?

He isn't ready to sleep.

Goodnight, good dog . . .

He likes those words,
the way they curl around him—
just like his moon-round bed.

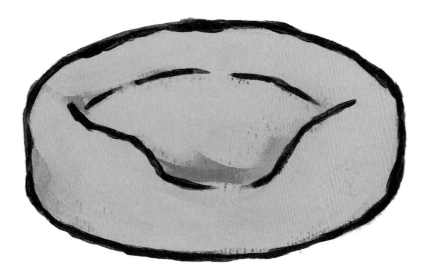

Except he's not sleepy. Not the dog.

But houses are. So houses sleep.

Children sleep.

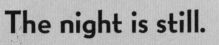

The night is still.

But the dog isn't sleepy.

Or only a little.

Just a little.

Maybe he can dream back the sun?

Then he might go to sleep.

So the dog makes himself snug

and says to himself, *Goodnight, good dog.*

Then he closes his eyes—
and soon he *has* dreamed the sun.

So he dreams some blue sky.

He dreams some green grass.

And then?

Someone is saying,

Good morning, good dog!

Because a new day is waiting.